I0830765

Author

Andrew Valkauskas

Artist

Vincent Pompetti

Producer & Layout

Andrew Valkauskas

Editing & Proofing

Sofia De Moura

Erik Growen

ISBN: 978-1-988051-26-0

SKOLL AND HATI'S APPETITES INITIATED RAGNAROK, AND FIMBULWINTER HAS SHOWN US NO MERCY. WE HAVE SURVIVED NINE MONTHS OF ETERNAL NIGHT AND UNENDING WINTER. LAKES AND RIVERS HAVE FROZEN OVER, FARMING IS BUT A DREAM, AND HUMANITY FIGHTS FOR SURVIVAL.

ONLY FOOLS TRAVEL OVERLAND. THE ROADS ARE LITTERED WITH THIEVES WHO ARE OUT TO STEAL IN ORDER TO SURVIVE. TRAVELING BY SHIP IS EASIER, BUT ON THIS DAY, I WOULD RATHER AVOID IT, FOR I CARRY WITH ME SOMETHING OF TREMENDOUS VALUE.

MY NAME IS VARGEISA, VERY FEW KNOW ME BY MY REAL NAME...
MY ENEMIES CALL ME THE "FIRE WOLF".

TODAY, I RATHER BE NAMELESS, I NEED TO REACH ISLANDIA WITHOUT ANY COMPLICATION, HOWEVER, THOSE TROUBLESOME NORNS, THE SPINNERS OF "FATE"...HAVE IT IN FOR ME.

I WASN'T GOING TO BE TRAVELLING ALONE...
...AND THIS BUNCH LOOK LIKE THEY'VE STAINED THEIR HANDS WITH BLOOD BEFORE

THE NIGHT WAS CALM AT FIRST, BUT THEN THE SEA GREW ANGRY... OBJECTING TO OUR WESTWARD JOURNEY.

I QUICKLY FORGOT ABOUT MY DUBIOUS COMPANIONS AS ONE BY ONE, THE SEA GRIPPED THEM IN HER VIOLENT EMBRACE

BRACE YOURSELVES FOR NJORD'S FURY!
FOLLOW ME... VANADIS, WHAT DO YOU SEE?

LORDS AND LADIES OF THE SEA. I AM VANADIS, DAUGHTER OF GROA. REVEAL YOUR WILL TO ME! PERMIT MY EYES TO PIERCE THE VEIL...
THE GODS ARE ANGRY... THE THUNDERER RIDES AGAINST US! VENGEANCE COMES!
SOMEONE HAS STOLEN FROM THE AESIR!
FREY'S BALLS! ARE YOU SHITTING ME?? THOR?!? WELL, IF MY TRAVELLING COMPANIONS WEREN'T ALREADY AGAINST ME, THEY'RE GOING TO BE.

BUT BEFORE ANYONE CAN CONFRONT VARGEISA, THOR'S STORM DRIVES THE SHIP TOWARDS A DEADLY AND ROCKY SHORE!
VARGEISA UTTERS A PRAYER TO ANGRBODA...
CRACK!
...AND IN THE LAST MOMENT, A WAVE REDIRECTS THE SHIP

YOU ARE LUCKY TO BE ALIVE!
WELL YOU'RE NOT THE GUESTS WE'RE WAITING FOR. I'LL TAKE YOU TO OUR LORD. HE'LL FIGURE OUT WHAT TO DO WITH YOU.
WHO ARE THEY WAITING FOR?
THE HUSKARL WELCOMED US TO ATLOY... AN ISLAND OFF NORVEIG'S COAST. IT'S A SLAVER'S HUB. THE LORD'S NAME IS BARD AND HIS THRALLS ARE BUSY PREPARING FOR SOMEONE VERY IMPORTANT. BARD'S SECRETIVE AND HIS HOSPITALITY IS RELUCTANT AT BEST.
I MUST EXCUSE MYSELF, BUT MY RIGHT HAND BALDRI WILL TAKE CARE OF YOU.
THE STORM OUTSIDE IS ONLY GETTING WORSE. I THINK WE'RE HERE FOR THE NIGHT, AND IT'S COZY IN HERE.
I'M BALDRI. DON'T TAKE OFF YOUR CLOAKS. THERE'S NO ROOM IN THE MEAD HALL FOR YOU. FOLLOW ME.

FREY'S NUTS IT'S COLD! WELL, WE MIGHT AS WELL MAKE THE MOST OF IT. MY NAME IS SIGYN, AND DON'T WORRY MY FRIENDS AND I DON'T BITE.
WELL MET! MY NAME'S KALLA AND I THINK WE WERE BOTH HEADED TO ISLANDIA, BUT THE GODS HAD OTHER PLANS FOR US TONIGHT.
THE FIRE'S STARTED SO WE WON'T FREEZE. MY NAME'S JOKUL AND I'M A GALDR. MY RUNE MAGIC COMES IN HANDY, EH VANADIS?
ALWAYS THE BRAGGART. SURE, SOMETIMES YOUR RUNE MAGIC WILL BE MORE USEFUL THAN MY SEITH MAGIC BUT FJORI WILL PROBABLY DISAGREE...?
YOU KNOW IT VANADIS! UNLIKE YOUR DREARY SPIRIT MAGIC, MY SPELL SONGS PUT A SMILE ON EVERYONE'S FACE... WELL EXCEPT MAYBE TURBOG...
THE MAN NAMED TURBOG WAS RIGHT, NOTHING ABOUT THIS CHAIN OF EVENTS FELT RIGHT.
MUCH LIKE THE ALL FATHER, I TRAVEL UNDER MANY GUISES, AND TONIGHT "KALLA" WILL SUIT ME WELL.
JUST THEN, BALDRI ESCORTED A RICHLY DRESSED MAN AND HIS ENTOURAGE INTO THE TENT.
SILENCE! I HEAR SOMEONE COMING. INCREDIBLE! ANOTHER SHIP SURVIVED THIS STORM. BE ON YOUR GUARD THIS NIGHT FEELS... UNNATURAL.

WELCOME TO ATLOY. I WILL HAVE TO ASK YOU TO JOIN OUR OTHER UNEXPECTED GUESTS IN THE OVERFLOW TENT. COME AND MEET THE OTHERS WHO SURVIVED THE STORM AND LANDED ON OUR SHORES.
THE NEW GUESTS WERE HALF A DOZEN MEN, EVERYONE OF THEM ARMED. THEY WERE LED BY A VERY SHORT MAN WITH SHREWD EYES.
HIS COMPANION WAS PERHAPS THE BIGGEST MAN I HAD EVER LAID EYES ON. THERE WAS A WILD QUALITY ABOUT HIM THAT PUT US ALL ON EDGE. I SMELL TROLL BLOOD, BUT WHO AM I TO JUDGE?

WELL MET! I AM OLVIR, THE BIG FELLA IS EGIL, AND THESE FINE WARRIORS ARE SVEN AND OLAF.
I AM A TAX COLLECTOR UNDER THE EMPLOY OF CHIEFTAIN THORIR, AND THIS STORM HAS BLOWN ME WAY OFF COURSE. IT IS BY PURE FORTUNE THAT WE DID NOT DROWN ON THIS NIGHT.
I WOULDN'T LET MY LITTLE MOUSE DROWN!
IT WOULD TAKE MUCH MORE THAN A STORM TO STOP A SKALLAGRIMMSSON.
THIS IS NO ORDINARY STORM, I SENSE SEITH MAGIC ALL AROUND. SOMEONE POWERFUL IS COMING...
MAGIC YOU SAY? THEN WE RAISE OUR DRINKING HORNS TO BRAGI AND FACE IT HEAD ON WITH A FIERY HEART AND A FULL BELLY!

THE BREAD IS STALE AND THE WINE HAS BEEN WATERED DOWN- WHAT KIND OF HOST WOULD INSULT US LIKE THIS?!

BALDRI LEAVES ONCE MORE TOWARDS THE DOCKS... MORE UNEXPECTED GUESTS?

THE STORM HAS INTENSIFIED.

ANOTHER FOOT OF SNOW SINCE WE ARRIVED.

THERE ARE FOUR NEW SHIPS AT THE DOCKS.

THEY APPEAR TO HAVE NO DAMAGE FROM THE STORM.

LOOK SHARP! LOOKS LIKE THE OFFICIAL GUESTS HAVE ARRIVED.

OUT OF THE NEWLY ARRIVED SHIPS, COME OUT OVER A HUNDRED MEN, MOST ARE SOLDIERS, BUT SOME APPEAR TO BE COURT DIPLOMATS.

AT THE HEAD, A ROYAL PAIR APPROACH - A KING AND QUEEN.

IT IS KING ERIK BLOOD-AXE AND QUEEN GUNNHILD.

HE EARNED HIS MONICKER FROM THE MANY SIBLINGS HE KILLED IN THE PURSUIT OF HIS LATE FATHER'S THRONE - THE HIGH KING OF ALL OF NORVEIG.

AS THEY PASS BY US IN THE TENT, THE QUEEN'S GAZE RESTS ON EACH OF OUR FACES. SHE NOT ONLY LOOKS ME IN THE EYE BUT ALSO AT THE BUNDLE I HAVE TRIED TO HIDE...

EASY... CALM DOWN EGIL

CRACK!

...LIKE I SAID, THE NORNS HATE ME.

HEY WE SHOULD SNEAK IN THERE, WITH SO MANY PEOPLE THEY WON'T EVEN NOTICE US
HA HA! YEAH!
EGIL, CAN I COUNT ON YOU TO BEHAVE IN THERE?
I AGREE WITH VANADIS, BUT I HAVE A FEELING THAT IF WE DON'T GO IN, FATE WILL BRING THAT SORCERESS QUEEN GUNNHILD TO US. WE MAY AS WELL BE WARM IF OUR PATHS ARE TO CROSS.
I FELT GREAT SEITH MAGIC EMANATING FROM THE QUEEN. SHE HAS TORMENTED SOULS READY TO DO HER BIDDING. I SAY WE STAY HERE, I DON'T LIKE OUR ODDS IN THERE.
I MUST KEEP IT HIDDEN.
THEN IT IS SETTLED, WE DRINK AND FEAST INSIDE, HA!

EVERYONE MUST BE WATCHING KING ERIK, BUT IT'S QUEEN GUNNHILD WHO'S THE REAL THREAT TO MY JOURNEY.
I WILL PLEDGE MY LOYALTY TO YOUR HUSBAND, BUT I WANT ASSURANCES.
WHAT KIND?
WHY ARE THEY HERE? THE KING IS BUSY DRINKING, BUT THE QUEEN....
WITH THE COMING OF FIMBULWINTER, OUR CROPS FAILED AND WE WERE FORCED TO EAT OUR COWS AND GOATS.
IF WE GRANT THIS, THEN YOU MUST OPENLY DENOUNCE ALL THE OTHER CLAIMANTS TO NORVEIG'S HIGH THRONE. YOU MUST NOT ONLY PLEDGE YOUR LOYALTY, BUT ALSO YOUR SWORD. NONE OF ERIK'S HALF-BROTHERS, HALF-SISTERS AND COUSINS CAN HAVE A LEGITIMATE CLAIM. YOU WILL SWEAR THIS ON MY HUSBAND'S OATH RING.
I HAVE TRANSFORMED OUR ISLAND INTO A SLAVE TRADING MARKET. IF YOU GIVE US PROTECTION, STATUS AND MONOPOLY, WE WILL SEND YOU VAST SUMS IN TAXATION.
I ACCEPT YOUR TERMS.
THEN WE ARE IN AGREEMENT! NO MORE BORING NEGOTIATIONS, I GO DRINK AND CELEBRATE WITH MY MEN. GUNNHILD, YOU CAN HANDLE ANY DETAILS...

UH OH, A DRUNK EGIL AND SYGIN HAVE JOINED THE TABLE OF HONOUR.
BY LOKI'S BLOOD, THEY WILL GET THEMSELVES ARRESTED, OR MAYBE KILLED!
NO... EGIL IS CLEARLY MOCKING THE ROYALS...
...AND THE QUEEN IS FIGHTING TO KEEP HER COMPOSURE.
OH NO, GUNNHILD SPOTTED ME!
THERE IS ONE MORE THING...
TONIGHT FALLS UPON THE DISABLOTT, THE ANNUAL SACRIFICE TO BELEYGR THE ISLAND'S LAND VAETTIR. DESPITE THE STORM, I PLAN TO GO, SINCE IF WE DO NOT APPEASE OUR LAND SPIRIT, WE MAY BE FACED WITH MORE HARDSHIPS IN THE COMING YEAR. BELEYGR IS A FICKLE LAND SPIRIT, SO PLEASE DO NOT FEEL INSULTED IF I LEAVE THE HALL FOR A SHORT PERIOD.
APPEASING YOUR ISLAND'S LAND SPIRIT IS OF UTMOST IMPORTANCE, AND I HAVE YEARS OF EXPERIENCE WITH THE CORRECT RITUALS AND INCANTATIONS THAT WOULD PLEASE SUCH A LAND VAETTIR. ALLOW ME TO GO IN YOUR PLACE, AFTER ALL, YOU HAVE UNRULY GUESTS THAT MUST BE DEALT WITH.

I WOULD BE HONOURED TO HAVE YOUR MAJESTY PERFORM THE DISABLOT, WHILE I DEAL WITH THE UNRULY GUESTS.

SHE WHISPERS IN BARD'S EAR...

I KNOW THE OAF THAT SHIPWRECKED UPON YOUR SHORES.

...AND SLIPS HIM A SOLUTION TO HIS PROBLEMS?

YOU SIX ARE COMING WITH ME.
SHE THEN DEMANDS THAT BALDRI JOIN THEM AND THAT HE BRING THREE SLAVES. NO ONE QUESTIONS HER, NO ONE. NOW SHE TURNS TO ME.

YOU TWO SHOULD COME. IT WOULD BE MOST DISRESPECTFUL IF YOU DID NOT THANK THE LAND VAETTIR FOR HIS GENEROUS HOSPITALITY THAT SAVED YOU FROM THE WINTER STORM AT SEA.
HOW COULD SHE KNOW? OLVIR CAN FEEL IT AS WELL, THIS WON'T END WELL.

THE QUEEN DOESN'T WAIT FOR US, THE STORM STRENGTHENS.
TURBOG TAKES THE LEAD, HIS TRACKING SKILLS WILL BE HELPFUL.
WE CANNOT SEE THEM AT ALL, JUST THEIR FOOTSTEPS.
WE'RE NOT ALONE!

IT'S OBVIOUS THAT THIS WARBAND HAS FOUGHT TOGETHER BEFORE.
THEY STAND BACK-TO-BACK WITHOUT SAYING A WORD.
...OLVIR AND I FOLLOW SUIT
JOKULL SCRIBES A MYSTIC RUNE ON HIS ARROWS, ENSURING THAT THEY HIT THEIR MARK.
TURBOG IS A MAN POSSESSED BY SUPERNATURAL RAGE.
AS SHE SNAPS A BONE IN HER HANDS...
SNAP!
SNAP!
VANADIS SUMMONS THE SPIRITS TO HER SIDE.
...THE WOLVES HOWL IN PAIN.

STRANGE... HOW DID WOLVES GET ON THIS ISLAND?
THERE'S MAGIC AT PLAY HERE.
MEANWHILE ATOP THE MOUNTAIN A GREAT WELL SITS AT THE BASE OF AN ANCIENT ASH TREE.
BALDRI LEADS THE SLAVES TO THE BOUGHS.
BELEYGR. BELEYGR! HEAR ME! LORD BARD HAS BROUGHT YOU AN OFFERING ON THIS SOLSTICE.

WE ARRIVE LATE, THE RITUAL HAS BEGUN.
SHE IS SURPRISED TO SEE US.
BUT HER COMPOSURE RETURNS.

AS AGREED UPON BY OUR ANCESTORS WITH YOU, BENEVOLENT LAND VAETTIR, WE GIVE YOU YOUR BLOT!

FETCH A BRANCH FROM THE SACRED ASH.
AS AGREED UPON BY OUR ANCESTORS WITH YOU, BENEVOLENT LAND VAETTIR, WE GIVE YOU YOUR BLOT!
BELEYGR! CONSUME THE OFFERING WE BRING FORTH IN YOUR NAME!
SHE SPLASHES US WITH THE SLAVE BLOOD.
IT IS DONE!
YOU ARE LATE! YOU OFFEND BELEYGR BY ARRIVING AT THE END OF THE CEREMONY. I DO NOT WANT TO HEAR EXCUSES. TO MAKE AMENDS, YOU WILL STAY AND TAKE DOWN THE OFFERING FROM THE TREE. BARD AND I ARE LEAVING, WE WILL SEE YOU BACK IN THE GREAT FEASTING HALL.

MEANWHILE BACK AT THE MEAD HALL.
LET'S PLAY "OATH, TOAST, OR BOAST"... YOU GO FIRST!
I TOAST THE KING AND QUEEN, MAY THEY RULE OVER A SMALL ISLAND AND HAVE MANY VASSALS OF CRABS AND FISH! HAW HAW HAW!
EGIL, LET'S BURY THE BAD BLOOD BETWEEN YOU AND THE ROYALS. I BRING YOU MEAD ON THEIR BEHALF.
JARL BARD FOLLOWED THE QUEEN'S INSTRUCTIONS.
EGIL WAS OBVIOUSLY SUSPICIOUS.
BEING A TRAINED GALDR, HE TRACED A MYSTIC RUNE WITH HIS FINGER, REVEALING THE POISON WITHIN THE BREW.

I WOULD LIKE TO PROPOSE AN OATH THAT OUR HOST WILL BE VISITED BY THE NORNS AND HIS FATE PAID IN FULL WHAT IT IS DUE FOR HIS HOSPITALITY HERE TONIGHT!
JARL BARD STEPS OUTSIDE FOR A BREATH OF FRESH AIR.

ALRIGHT, LET'S GET THIS DONE. TAKE THEM DOWN AND BURY THEM.
UGH, WHY'S HE STILL MOVING?! HE'S SUPPOSED TO BE DEAD!
THERE'S A LOT OF MOVEMENT DOWN THERE!
DROP HIM!
WHATEVER IT IS, IT'S GETTING LOUDER.
DRAUGAR!
RUN!!!!
THE STORM, THE WOLVES, NOW THIS... GUNNHILD KNOWS WHAT I CARRY.
THE POWER REQUIRED TO CONTROL THIS HORDE IS BEYOND ME.

THE RED-HEADED WOMAN WHO WENT TO THE PEAK WITH US...
...ARREST HER FOR THE MURDER.
LIES! I SAW IT ALL, IT WAS EGIL WHO KILLED THE JARL.
EGIL?! THEN ARREST THIS WOMAN! SHE WAS DRINKING WITH HIM.
IF THEY STILL LIVE, BRING THEM TO ME, THE RED-HAIRED WOMAN IS KNOWN AS THE "FIRE WOLF". DO NOT LET HER ESCAPE.
"FIRE WOLF"? THE QUEEN OBVIOUSLY WANTS TO PIN THE CRIME ON YOU. YOU SHOULD GO. I HAVE A FEELING EGIL IS IN TROUBLE, GO AND FIND HIM.
WE HAVE TO GO AND CLEAR SYGIN'S NAME.
AGREED, WE SHOULD GO TO CONFRONT THE KING AND QUEEN.
I DEPARTED TO FIND EGIL. MAY THE NORNS BE MERCIFUL.

...THE REDHEAD WHO TRAVELS WITH YOU... IS SHE DEAD?
NO
IT WAS EGIL!
I WANT EGIL'S HEAD!
IF IT WAS EGIL, THEN I WILL BRING HIM HERE PEACEFULLY
SYGIN IS INNOCENT, RELEASE HER.
IF HE IS GUILTY, THEN I WILL PAY A WEREGILD FOR THE DEATH HE CAUSED.
IF YOU WANT SYGIN TO BE FREED, AND YOU WANT EGIL ALIVE, THEN YOU WILL BRING ME THE FIRE WOLF... DEAD OR ALIVE.
"SHE CARRIES A CURSE, A CURSE THAT HAS BROUGHT THESE EVIL EVENTS TO ATLOY. KILL HER AND BRING ME HER BELONGINGS AND I WILL LET YOU LIVE."

A SMALL FISHING TOWN BURNS, ITS CITIZENS ARE BUTCHERED BY EGIL...

THOSE ARE NOT FISHERMEN, BUT DRAUGAR, THE UNDEAD WE SAW AT THE WELL!

THEY COME FOR ME, SENSING ME AT A DISTANCE.

WHAT?!
THEY SEEK WHAT I CARRY!

EGIL!
THEY STOLE
MY SATCHEL!

THEY ARE BREAKING OFF THEIR ATTACK
HELP ME EGIL! GUNNHILD IS HERE.
I DO NOT SEE THE ARRIVAL OF THE OTHERS
VANADIS, STOP HER!
...BUT EGIL DOES.
NO! WE MUST HELP HER.
EGIL IS RIGHT!
BRING ME WHAT SHE CARRIES!
HER DARK CHILDREN FROM THE GRAVE ARE LEGION ...
ALONE I WILL BE SWALLOWED BY THE DARK TIDE.

...BUT I DO NOT FIGHT ALONE!
GUNNHILD'S POWER IS TERRIFYING
...VANADIS WIELDS BUT A FRACTION.
BUT TOGETHER WE RETRIEVE MY PRIZED SATCHEL.
...AND HER DRAUGAR FALL.
YOUR LIVES FOR THE SEAL. GIVE IT TO ME!
WE'VE WON, YOU CANNOT STOP MY DESTINY!

WRONG! MY ARMY IS ETERNAL. RISE CHILDREN OF THE HANGED GOD!
RUN!
WE CANNOT WIN THIS FIGHT.

...BUT THE WAR IS FAR FROM OVER. WITH MY NEW WARBAND WE SAIL TO ISLANDIA.
LOKI, I AM COMING!

Eyrbyggja Saga
graphic novels

Fate of the Norns: Ragnarok
role-playing games

The Illuminated Edda
mythology books

Gulveig
card games

PENDELHAVEN PUBLISHING

www.ingramcontent.com/pod-product-compliance
Lightning Source LLC
Chambersburg PA
CBHW041427300726
48981CB00008B/424